This book
belongs to:

_____

MESSAGE TO PARENTS

This book is perfect for parents and children to read aloud together. First read the story to your child. When you read it again, run your finger under each line, stopping at each picture for your child to "read." Help your child to figure out the picture. If your child makes a mistake, be encouraging as you say the right word. Point out the written word beneath each picture in the margin on the page. Soon your child will be "reading" aloud with you, and at the same time learning the symbols that stand for words.

Library of Congress Cataloging-in-Publication Data

Schorsch, Kit.
    Stone soup / retold by Kit Schorsch ; illustrated by Pat Schories.
        p.   cm. — (A Read along with me book)
    Summary: Retells in rebus format the classic tale in which all the townspeople share a delicious soup that started out as a stone and water.
    ISBN 0-02-898167-7
    [1. Folklore—France.   2. Rebuses.]   I. Schories, Patricia, ill. II. Title.   III. Series.
PZ8.1.S356St   1989
398.2'1'0944—dc19
[E]
                                                                89-589
                                                                CIP
                                                                AC

Stone Soup

A Read Along With Me Book

Retold by **Kit Schorsch**
Illustrated by **Pat Schories**

CHECKERBOARD PRESS
NEW YORK

soldier

village

food

door

Once, in a far land, a was

traveling home from a war. After

many days he came to a .

"Perhaps I can get some

here," he said to himself. So he

knocked at the of the first

he came to. The was

opened by a .

"Please," said the , "I have

been traveling for many days and

I am very hungry. Have you a

little  to spare—maybe some

 or ? Anything would

be good."

The  shook his head. He

knew a hungry could eat all

the  he had in the 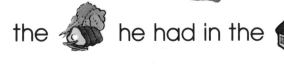 .

house

man

meat

beans

man

food

soldier

house

village

"I am sorry," said the .

"I am poor and have no

to spare."

So the tried at the next

 , and the next, and the

next, until he reached the last

 in the . But at each

 the people said the same

thing: they were poor and had

no to spare. Then the

sat down and thought.

After a while he called all the people into the square. "We are all poor," he said, "and I am hungry. So I will make soup for us all."

stone

stone

woman

village

" soup?" asked an old

 . "I am the best cook in this

 and I have never heard

of soup! No one in this part

of the country has ever heard

of soup."

"It is not difficult to make," said

the . "But I will need a large

 ."

Some were sent to fetch

the . The gathered

firewood, and the built a big

 . The was filled with

water. The put it on the

 . "Now we need a ,"

said the . "Not too big and

not too small—a good solid ."

soldier

pot

children

women

men

fire

stone

village

children

soldier

pot

"A  ! We certainly have plenty of those," said the mayor. "Even in our poor  ."

All the  ran off to find a good solid  . They brought back many different shapes and sizes. At last the  said,

"This  is just right. Not too big and not too small–a good solid  ." And with that he dropped the  into the

of hot water. " soup always

tastes better with a little salt and

pepper," said the 🎩 as he

started to stir the soup.

"Salt and pepper? We certainly

have that," said a 👩 , and sent

her 👨‍👩‍👧 to bring some. The

woman

soldier

stone

pot

men

women

 added a little of each. "It looks like we have picked a good ," said the . He leaned over the . "Hmmm, it smells very good." None of the or could smell anything. But they said nothing.

"It's too bad no one has ," said the  . "  help to make soup truly delicious."

"I can spare some  ," said a  , and he ran to get them.

When he got back he quickly dropped the  into the 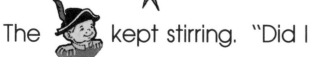 .

The kept stirring. "Did I mention ?" he said. "  soup without  is hardly soup."

"But," he sighed, "it's just as well.

No one has any to spare."

"We do," said a . "I know

we do. If they will help the

soup I will get them right away."

She told her  to run to

their and fetch the .

The came back very quickly,

and they carefully dropped the

 into the .

beans

stone

woman

children

house

pot

soldier

village

stones

"Yes," said the , stirring the

soup, "this is a good solid . It

will make fine soup. Your is

probably full of good , and

you never knew it." The

men

women

cabbage

potatoes

soldier

stone

woman

sniffed the soup again and smiled.

A few and did the

same.

"If only we had a little or a

few ," said the . "Then

we could fully bring out the fine

flavor of the ."

"Why, I have some and

 to spare," said a .

"So do I," said another, and off

they ran to get something to add

to the  soup. They were back

in a minute. The  stirred as

each proudly added her

 and to the .

" ," said the  , shaking

his head. "Yes, I can smell that

 is all this soup needs to

make it fit for a king. But what

does it matter? We are all poor.

And the  soup is cooking

very well without it."

pot

meat

meat	
man	
pot	
 soldier	
stone	

" ," said a . "I can

spare some ." And off he ran.

He was back almost at once, and

dropped the into the .

The soup was bubbling, and it

smelled very good. At last the

soup was ready. Everyone

brought a bowl, and the

shared it evenly. It was delicious!

"Amazing," said the mayor. "This

tasty soup from an old !

I would never have guessed it."

"Nor we," agreed all the people.

And they told the he would

be welcome in their if ever

he happened to pass that way

again.

village

Words I can read

- ☐ beans
- ☐ cabbage
- ☐ carrots
- ☐ children
- ☐ door
- ☐ fire
- ☐ food
- ☐ house

- ☐ man
- ☐ meat
- ☐ men
- ☐ pot
- ☐ potatoes
- ☐ soldier
- ☐ stone

- ☐ stones
- ☐ village
- ☐ woman
- ☐ women